Title I 1998-9

The Relatives Came

Story by CYNTHIA RYLANT

Illustrated by STEPHEN GAMMELL

Aladdin Paperbacks

Aladdin Paperbacks. An imprint of Simon & Schuster Children's Publishing Division. 1230 Avenue of the Americas, New York, NY 10020.
Text copyright © 1985 by Cynthia Rylant. Illustrations copyright © 1985 by Stephen Gammell. All rights reserved including the right
of reproduction in whole or in part in any form. First Aladdin Paperbacks edition, 1993. Printed in the United States of America. Also
available in a hardcover edition from Simon & Schuster Books for Young Readers.
10 9 8
The text of this book is set in 16 pt. Benguiat Book Condensed. The illustrations are rendered in colored pencil, reproduced in full color.

Library of Congress Cataloging-in-Publication Data
Rylant, Cynthia.
    The relatives came / story by Cynthia Rylant; illustrated by Stephen Gammell. — 1st Aladdin Books ed.
      p.   cm.
    Summary: The relatives come to visit from Virginia and everyone has a wonderful time.
    ISBN 0-689-71738-5
  [1. Family life—Fiction.] I. Gammell, Stephen, ill. II. Juvenile Collection (Library of Congress) III. Title.
PZ7.R982Re   1993
(E)—dc20   92-41394

For Aunt Agnes Little and her brood,

Dick Jackson and his, Gerry and ours

It was in the summer of the year when the relatives came.
They came up from Virginia. They left when their grapes
were nearly purple enough to pick, but not quite.

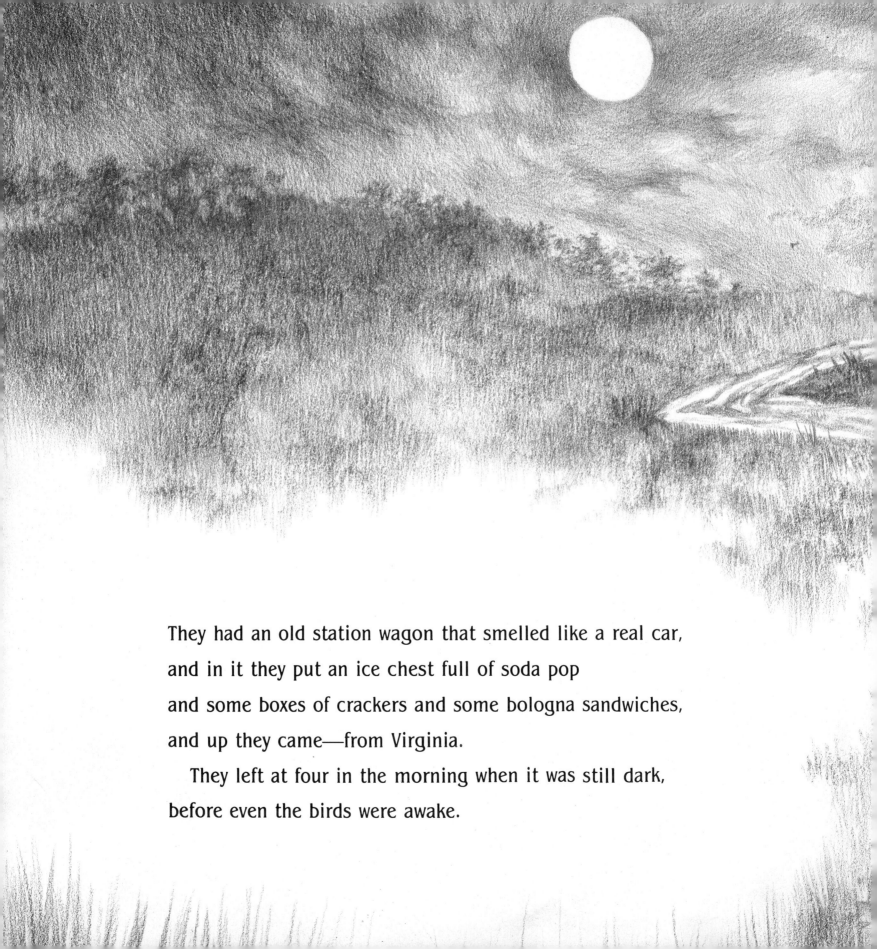

They had an old station wagon that smelled like a real car,
and in it they put an ice chest full of soda pop
and some boxes of crackers and some bologna sandwiches,
and up they came—from Virginia.

They left at four in the morning when it was still dark,
before even the birds were awake.

They drove all day long and into the night, and while they
traveled along they looked at the strange houses
and different mountains and they thought
about their almost purple grapes back home.
They thought about Virginia—
but they thought about us, too. Waiting for them.

So they drank up all their pop
and ate up all their crackers
and traveled up all those miles until finally
they pulled into our yard.

Then it was hugging time. Talk about hugging!

Those relatives just passed us all around their car, pulling us

against their wrinkled Virginia clothes, crying sometimes.

They hugged us for hours.

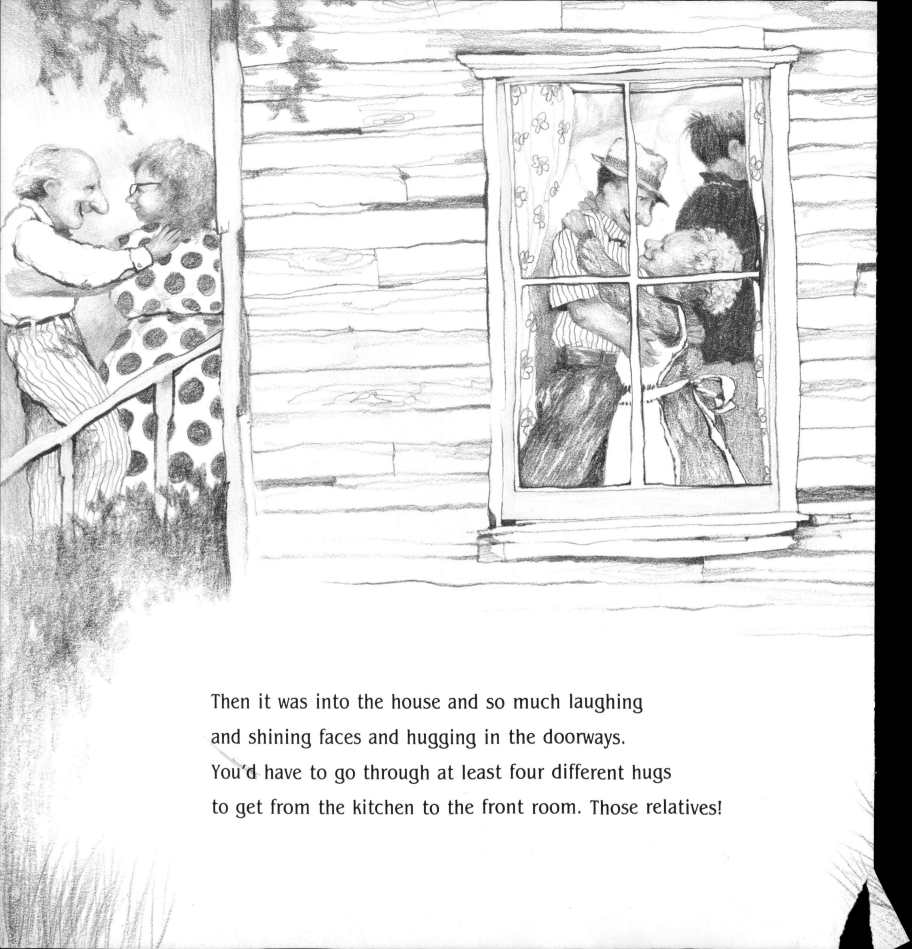

Then it was into the house and so much laughing
and shining faces and hugging in the doorways.
You'd have to go through at least four different hugs
to get from the kitchen to the front room. Those relatives!

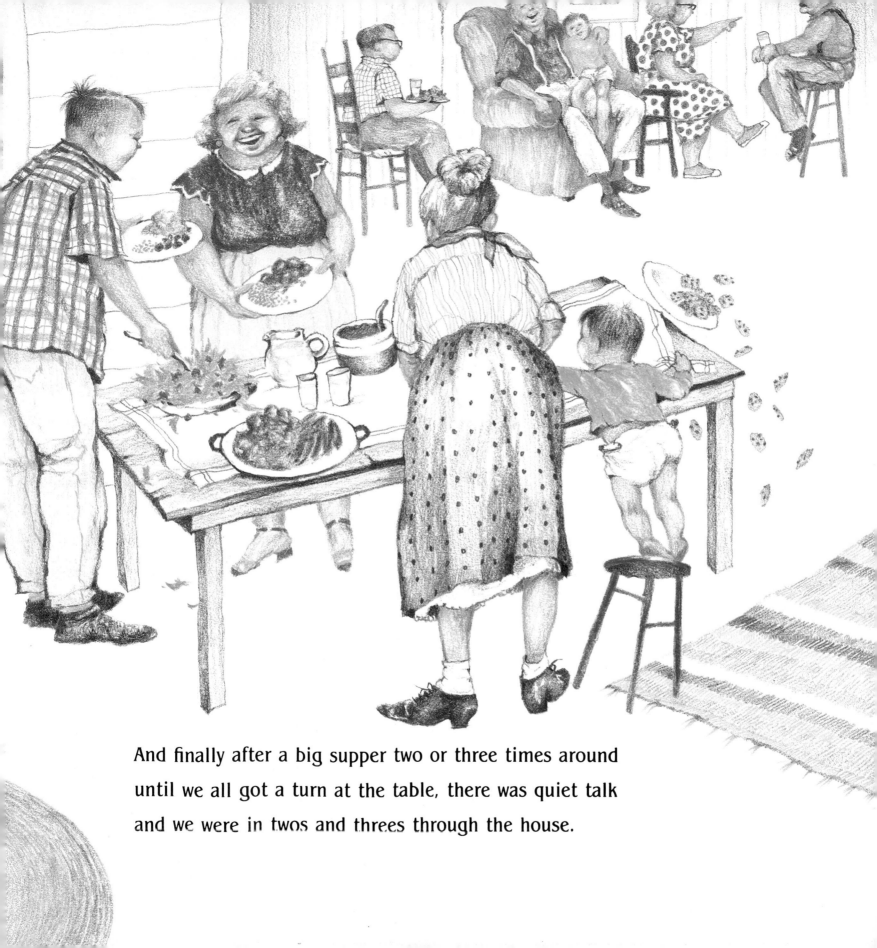

And finally after a big supper two or three times around
until we all got a turn at the table, there was quiet talk
and we were in twos and threes through the house.

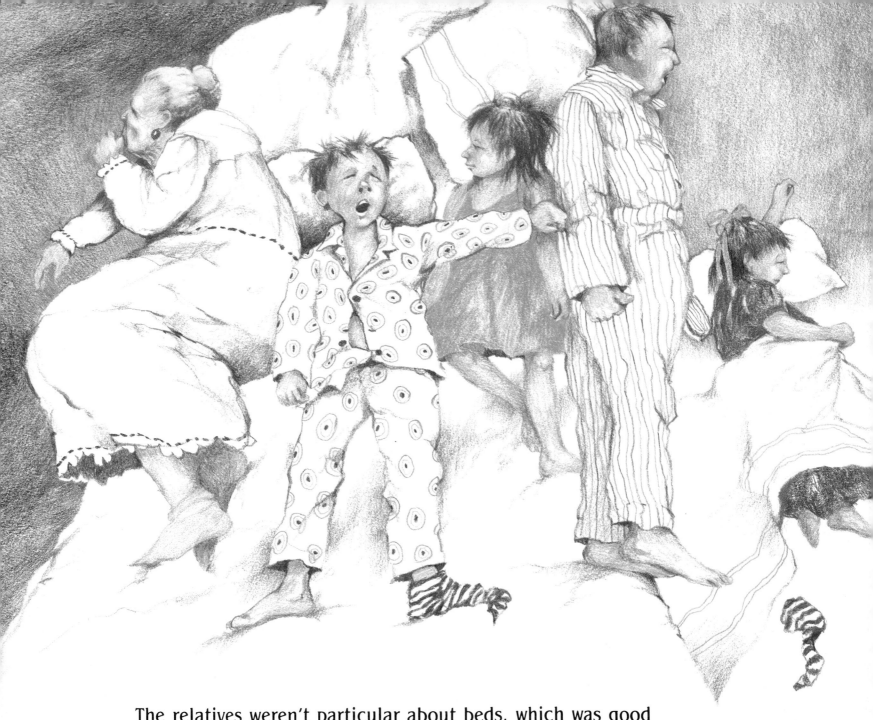

The relatives weren't particular about beds, which was good
since there weren't any extras, so a few squeezed in with us
and the rest slept on the floor, some with their arms
thrown over the closest person, or some with an arm across one person
and a leg across another.

It was different, going to sleep with all that new breathing in the house.

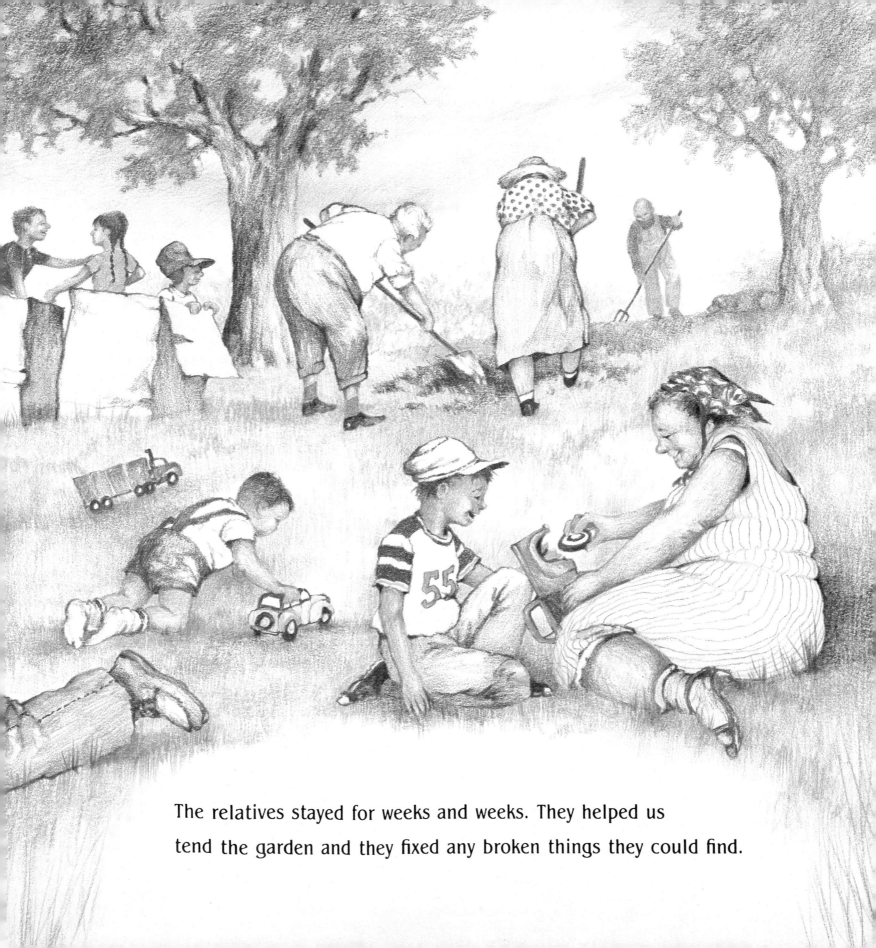

The relatives stayed for weeks and weeks. They helped us
tend the garden and they fixed any broken things they could find.

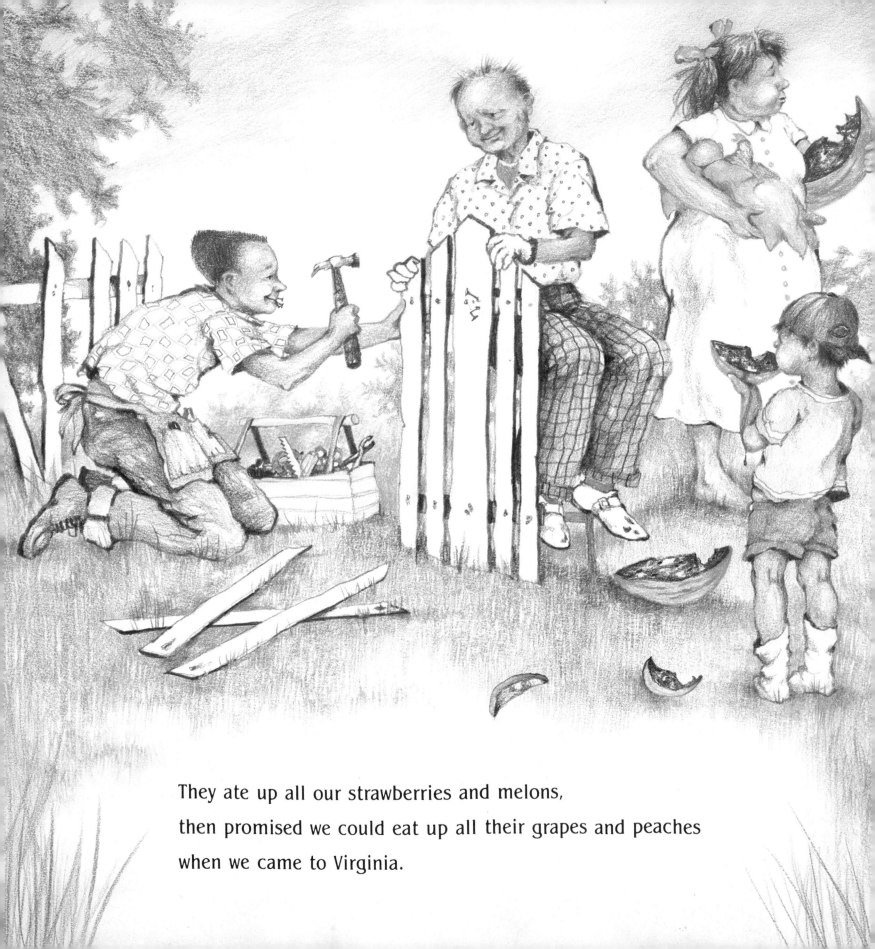

They ate up all our strawberries and melons,
then promised we could eat up all their grapes and peaches
when we came to Virginia.

But none of us thought about Virginia much. We were so busy
hugging and eating and breathing together.

Finally, after a long time, the relatives loaded up their ice chest

and headed back to Virginia at four in the morning.

We stood there in our pajamas and waved them off in the dark.

   We watched the relatives disappear down the road,

then we crawled back into our beds that felt too big and too quiet.

We fell asleep.

And the relatives drove on, all day long and into the night,
and while they traveled along they looked
at the strange houses and different mountains
and they thought about their dark purple grapes
waiting at home in Virginia.

But they thought about us, too. Missing them. And they missed us.

And when they were finally home in Virginia,
they crawled into their silent, soft beds and dreamed
about the next summer.